STAR WARS™

THE BATTLE OF ENDOR

W9-CIG-116

WRITTEN BY ELLA PATRICK

ART BY TOMATOFARM

AND POWERSTATION STUDIOS

DISNEP

LUCASFILM

PRESS

Los Angeles · New York

The galaxy was at war.
The evil Empire was building
a dangerous weapon called
a Death Star.
The giant space station floated
above the Forest Moon of Endor.
But the heroes of the
Rebel Alliance had a plan to
destroy the weapon, defeat the
Empire, and save the galaxy.

Jedi Knight Luke Skywalker traveled to Endor with his friends C-3PO, R2-D2, Leia, Han, and Chewbacca.
They met the furry Ewoks of Endor.

The Rebel Alliance needed the Ewoks' help to defeat the Empire. But first Luke had another mission that he had to face alone.

Luke gave himself up to
Darth Vader. He was Luke's father.
He had once been a Jedi, too.

But Darth Vader fell to the
dark side and served the Empire.
Luke wanted to save his father
from the dark side.

Darth Vader took Luke to the
Death Star to face the leader
of the Empire. The evil Emperor
wanted Luke to join the dark side.
But Luke refused.

Rebel Alliance ships arrived
to attack the Death Star.
But the Empire knew they were
coming. Imperial TIE fighters
began to attack the rebel ships!

Admiral Ackbar warned the rebel
pilots: "It's a trap!"
They were outnumbered
by the Empire's ships.
But the rebels didn't give up.
They kept fighting!

Han and Leia needed to destroy
the shield generator on Endor
that protected the Death Star.
But they were caught
by Imperial stormtroopers!

Suddenly, Ewoks began to
attack the troopers!
Han, Leia, and Chewbacca
broke free and joined the fight.

With the Death Star's shield
still working, the rebels
couldn't attack.

Then the superweapon
started firing on the rebel fleet!
Deadly blasts rocked their ships.

Rebel pilots Nien Nunb and Lando
were flying the *Millennium Falcon*.
They knew their friends on Endor
needed more time to take out
the shield generator.
The pilots had to keep fighting!

Luke was worried about
his friends, too.
He used the Force
to get his lightsaber.
He fought Darth Vader!

On Endor, Han, Leia, R2-D2, and C-3PO were trying to find a way to destroy the shield generator.

Then Chewbacca arrived in a stolen Imperial AT-ST walker! They could use the AT-ST to finish their mission.

Luke knocked Darth Vader
to the ground.
Luke was letting his fear and anger
get the best of him, which was
just what the evil Emperor wanted.

Luke remembered that he was
there to save his father.
He was a Jedi Knight.
He would not fall to the dark side.
Luke threw his lightsaber
to the ground.

Below on Endor, the bunker that
held the Death Star's
shield generator exploded
with a fiery blast. *Kaboom!*
The rebel heroes and the Ewoks
had completed their mission!

The rebel pilots were finally able to attack the Death Star.

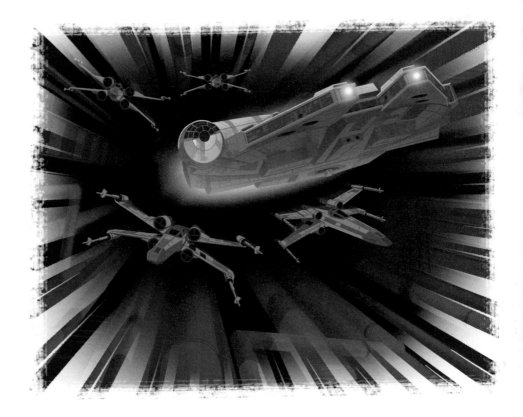

Rebel X-wings and the *Falcon* flew inside the space station. If they could destroy the Death Star's main reactor, the station would explode!

The Emperor was angry
that Luke refused to turn
to the dark side. He attacked.
Luke yelled in pain.
He needed help!

Suddenly, Luke's father
leapt into action.

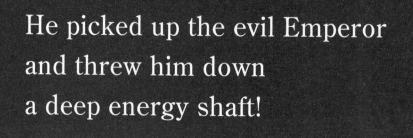

He picked up the evil Emperor
and threw him down
a deep energy shaft!

Luke removed his father's helmet.
He was badly hurt and would soon
become one with the Force.
He had turned away from the
dark side to save his son.

The rebel pilots finally reached
the Death Star's main reactor.
The ships blasted the reactor, and
the space station started to shake.
They needed to get out of there!

Luke and the rebel pilots made it
out of the Death Star just in time.

The superweapon exploded in a
shower of sparks!

Luke and his friends had worked together to defeat the Emperor and destroy the Death Star. The Rebel Alliance had saved the galaxy!